What Day is Today?

Written by
Sandy Parker

Illustrated by
Cathy Hofher

just think
BOOKS

*I thank Sondra Lewis whose help and guidance
each step of the way inspired me to make my
dream of writing children's books a reality!*

Text copyright © 2003 by Sandy Parker
Illustrations copyright © 2003 by Cathy Hofher

Cover Design by George Foster, Foster & Foster, Inc.
Interior Design by Mark NeuCollins, Neue Grafik Design Works

Published in United States of America by:

Just Think Books

Imprint of Canary Connect Publications
605 Holiday Road, Coralville, Iowa 52241-1016

Publisher's Cataloging-in-Publication
(Provided by Quality Books, Inc.)

Parker, Sandy (Sandra Norene), 1965-
    What day is today? / written by Sandy Parker ;
illustrated by Cathy Hofher.
    p. cm.
    SUMMARY: Animal illustrations help to introduce
    young children to the sequence of the days of the week
    and calendar through repetition and phonics.

    Audience: Ages 0-6.
    LCCN 2002106822
    ISBN 0-9643462-3-0

1. Calendar-Juvenile literature. 2. Days-Juvenile literature.
3. Week-Juvenile literature. [1. Calendar. 2. Days. 3. Week.]
I. Hofher, Cathy. II. Title.

CE85.P37 2003   529'.1
                        QBI33-586

Library Reinforced Binding   Acid-Free Paper
Printed in United States of America

For
Tyler
and
Paige -
Each Day Is A Gift!

s.p.

Today is Sunday,
the first day of the week.

Sunday	Monday	Tuesday	Wednesday	Thursday	Friday	Saturday

Today I saw
the shining sun.

Today is **Monday.**

Sunday	**Monday**	Tuesday	Wednesday	Thursday	Friday	Saturday

Today I saw
a monkey munching.

Today is Tuesday.

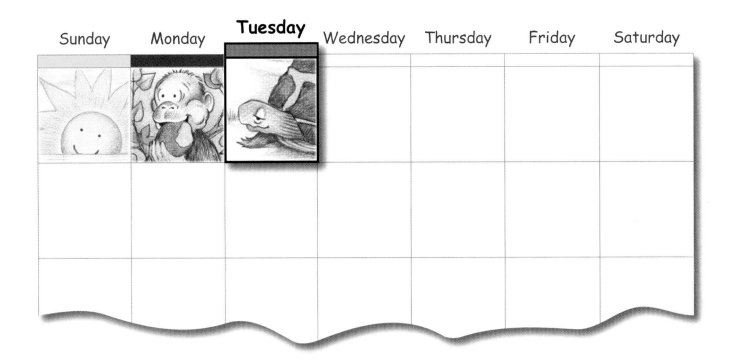

Sunday	Monday	**Tuesday**	Wednesday	Thursday	Friday	Saturday

Today I saw
a tired turtle.

Today is Wednesday.

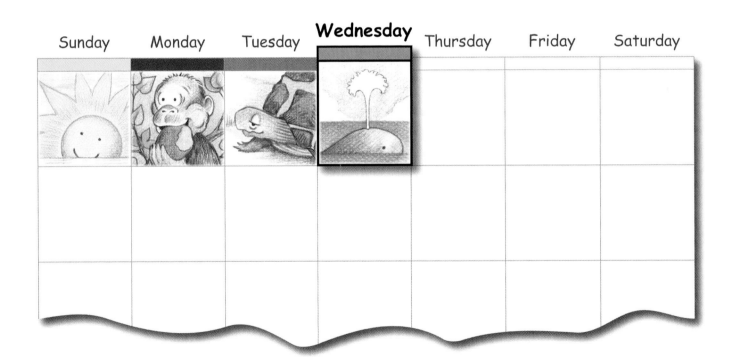

| Sunday | Monday | Tuesday | **Wednesday** | Thursday | Friday | Saturday |

Today I saw
a whale in the water.

Today is Thursday.

Today I saw
a thinking tiger.

Today is Friday.

| Sunday | Monday | Tuesday | Wednesday | Thursday | **Friday** | Saturday |

Today I saw
a fat frog.

Today is Saturday.

Sunday	Monday	Tuesday	Wednesday	Thursday	Friday	**Saturday**

Today I saw
a squirrel sitting.

What a wonderful
week I had!

Today is Sunday again.

Sunday	Monday	Tuesday	Wednesday	Thursday	Friday	Saturday

I wonder what
I'll see this week.

About the Author

Main Street Studio, North Liberty, IA

Sandy Parker loves encouraging children to use their imaginations. It was while she was playing outdoors with her young son and helping him to use his imagination that she conceived the idea for *What Day is Today?*

While taking coursework on emergent literacy Sandy discovered her interest in children's literature, especially how children begin to read and assimilate language. She has spent more than three years as a volunteer reading with children at the preschool and elementary levels.

She and her husband, Phil, a football coach, and their two children, Tyler and Paige, currently live in Coralville, Iowa. She is a Michigan native and has also lived in Ohio.

About the Illustrator

Cathy Hofher has been drawing since she was old enough to hold a pencil. The opportunity to combine her love of reading with art guided her towards a career as a children's book illustrator. She studied illustration at Ringling School of Art and has been a professional graphic designer and illustrator for 20 years.

The pictures in *What Day is Today?* are rendered in colored pencil. This is Cathy's third children's book.

A native of North Carolina, Cathy now lives in Williamsville, New York with her husband, Jim, a football coach, their three daughters, a cat, and a dog.

For fun, interactive ideas visit www.JustThinkBooks.com